P9-CRD-885

AN EXPLORER'S
GUIDE TO THE NETHER

AN EXPLORER'S GUIDE TO THE NETHER

LOST MINECRAFT JOURNALS BOOK TWO

Winter Morgan

Sky Pony Press
New York

Copyright © 2015 by Hollan Publishing, Inc.

Sky Pony Press books may be purchased in bulk at special discounts for
sales promotion, corporate gifts, fund-raising, or educational purposes.
Special editions can also be created to specifications. For details, contact
the Special Sales Department, Sky Pony Press, 307 West 36th Street,
11th Floor, New York, NY 10018 or info@skyhorsepublishing.com.

Sky Pony® is a registered trademark of Skyhorse Publishing, Inc.®,
a Delaware corporation.

Minecraft® is a registered trademark of Notch Development AB.
The Minecraft game is copyright © Mojang AB.

Visit our website at www.skyponypress.com.

10 9 8 7 6 5 4 3 2 1

Library of Congress Cataloging-in-Publication Data is available on file.

Cover photo by Megan Miller

Print ISBN: 978-1-5107-0351-3
Ebook ISBN: 978-1-5107-0354-4

Printed in Canada

TABLE OF CONTENTS

AN EXPLORER'S
GUIDE TO THE NETHER

1

PREPARATIONS AND PORTALS

'll make the portal," said Toby, "but I need some obsidian."

Harriet checked her inventory, then shook her head. "I don't have any. But before we travel to the Nether, shouldn't we read more of the journal? I know William might be there, but we should have a plan before we go. We could be walking into a trap."

Jack looked over at Julian. "Well, what does it say next?"

Julian was riffling through his bag and starting to panic. "It isn't in my inventory!"

"Where is it then?" asked Harriet.

Together they looked around the desert, searching the ground for the book in case Julian might have dropped it. They couldn't find anything though, and it looked like the journal really was gone.

"Wait a minute," said Oliver. "Ezra is missing."

Renewing their search, they called into the distance. "Ezra!"

There was no reply.

"Maybe he took the journal," said Toby.

Julian defended his friend. "I don't think Ezra would steal the journal. He's a good guy."

"Well, where is he then? Why didn't he tell us he was leaving?" Toby asked.

Julian was silent. He trusted his friend, but Toby was right—Ezra had left without telling them. As Julian stood without a response, a voice called out in the distance. "Help!"

"What was that?" asked Harriet.

"It's Ezra!" shouted Jack.

In the distance, Julian spotted Ezra in a portal. *Charles* stood beside him, holding Ezra in place. Purple mist rose around them, and they disappeared. "We need to help him!" Julian cried.

"I bet Charles stole the journal, too," said Harriet.

"You're probably right. There's no time to waste. We need to save Ezra," said Julian. "And maybe we can retrieve the journal, as well."

"We need to find more obsidian," Toby reminded him.

The group searched all of their inventories and found enough obsidian to make a portal. They passed through the portal, enveloped in purple mist. Within seconds they arrived in the Nether.

Harriet shuddered as she looked around. She didn't like being in the Nether and she hoped their visit would be short.

Julian broke the portal. He didn't want anyone following them. Then he looked out at the Nether landscape. He couldn't see Ezra or Charles nearby. "We're going to have to search for them. They could be anywhere."

Oliver was an expert at crafting maps and had charted many parts of the Nether, but when he spoke he sounded nervous. "I have no idea where we are. I think we're just going to have to walk around and make our own discoveries."

Harriet reassured Oliver. "I know you've been imprisoned for a long while and this is your first time exploring in ages, but we will find our way. We always do." Of course Harriet was also nervous, but she knew she had to be hopeful. Being nervous wasn't going to help anyone.

Toby and Jack led the way. They were confident in the Nether. Toby heard a noise and looked up at the sky. "Blazes!" he shouted.

"Snowballs!" called Jack.

The group grabbed as many snowballs as they could out of their inventories and began pelting the flying fiery mobs. Jack had perfect aim and destroyed one blaze in seconds. The other two blazes were harder to battle. They shot fireballs at the group, and Harriet only narrowly avoided being struck.

Julian threw a snowball. "Bull's-eye!" he called out when it destroyed the blaze.

As they battled the final blaze together, Julian noticed two people watching in the distance.

"I got it!" shouted Jack, skillfully destroying the final blaze and ready to celebrate.

Julian didn't congratulate Jack—he was too busy running toward the two people who were now passing by a lava waterfall.

"Where are you going?" Toby called out.

"I think I see Ezra and Charles!" Julian shouted back.

The gang followed Julian, sprinting toward the two people in the distance. When they got closer, they realized they had made a mistake. Ezra and Charles were nowhere to be seen. The two strangers took out their bows and shot arrows at the gang.

"Stop! Please don't shoot!" Julian called out.

"Don't come any closer," shouted a girl wearing a red helmet.

"We won't. We aren't here to harm you. We just thought you were someone else," Julian said.

The girl put down her bow, and told her friend to stop shooting arrows. "Why are you here? What's your purpose for traveling to the Nether?"

"We are looking for friends who are being kept prisoner here," Julian explained.

"The Nether is so large. How do you plan on finding them?" she asked, eyes darting across the group.

"We don't know, but we can't abandon our friends," said Julian.

"What is *your* purpose for traveling to the Nether?" Harriet asked the girl.

"We're treasure hunters. I'm Veronica."

The man with a green helmet spoke now, too. "I'm Valentino."

The gang introduced themselves. When it was Oliver's turn, Valentino studied him for a moment, then remarked, "You look very familiar. You kind of resemble the famous explorer Oliver."

"That's me," Oliver said proudly.

"That's impossible," said Valentino. "He's been missing for years. Nobody knows where he is."

"They found me," Oliver told Valentino, gesturing at the others. "I was being kept prisoner for years."

"What about William, your fellow explorer?" asked Veronica.

"That's who we are looking for," explained Oliver. "We're looking for him and another friend who we lost during our quest."

Jack was upset that Oliver had just told the strangers that they were searching for William. Veronica and Valentino were treasure hunters and to them William would be more valuable than a mine full of diamonds. This meant they would probably want to help them find William, and once they did find him, he would just be another treasure they could trade.

"You're searching for William? We want to join you," Valentino exclaimed.

Jack jumped in before Oliver could agree. "I think we're fine. We'd like to do this on our own."

Veronica smiled. "That's okay. We understand."

Jack didn't believe a word she said. As Veronica and Valentino walked away, he had a feeling this wouldn't be the last they saw of them.

A voice called out in the distance.

"Did you hear that?" asked Toby.

"Yes!" Julian was excited. It sounded like Ezra.

"Where is it coming from?"

Julian looked in every direction. He could hear the voice cry for help, but he couldn't see anyone.

"Look!" Harriet pointed to a book on the ground.

Julian picked it up. "It's William's second journal!"

"How did it get here?" asked Toby. "Could Charles have dropped it?"

"It doesn't matter," said Toby. "Just read it."

Julian flipped open the book and started to read.

2

JOURNAL ENTRY:
FEAR OF FIRE

Day 1: Solitude

I am stuck in a cell and I have no way to escape. I have searched through my inventory, but I don't have a pickaxe or a shovel. I am tired and I don't have any food left. I don't know how much longer I will survive here. After one attack, I worry that more blazes will spawn in this small room and I will be trapped with the fiery mobs. This wasn't how I imagined my life as an explorer. For the first time in my life, I dream of being saved by someone. I'm usually the resourceful one. I am the one who rescues other people. What have they done to me?

I'm also worried about Oliver. I wonder where he's being kept prisoner. I want to save him, but I can't even save myself.

I had a visitor today. There is a small hole in the wall and someone threw a carrot through it. It's enough food to keep me alive, but not enough to build up my energy and food bar.

I've been trying to figure out who is keeping me prisoner. When they dropped off the carrot ration, I shouted, "Who are you?"

A voice replied, "Who I am doesn't matter. Just eat your food. You will have a visitor soon enough, and they will explain everything."

"Who? Tell me more!" I pleaded.

Silence. There was no response. The visitor's deep voice had sounded sinister. My mind began to wander and I conjured up various images of the potential visitor. Was it Charles? Or Thao? Had they resurrected their blue army?

As my mind raced, a blaze spawned in the center of the room.

I jumped up. I was so scared. I hate fire. I was also a little shocked—I hadn't thought the cell was big enough for the horrific yellow creatures to spawn. But the cell must have been larger than nine by nine. I had nothing to help me, no snowballs in my inventory. It shot a fireball at me. And with no place to hide, I was hit. Hard.

I respawned in the bed, still a captive. Luckily the blaze was gone, but I was so very tired. My energy was at an all-time low.

A stranger entered the room.

"Who are you?" I asked. He wore a red shirt and jeans. He didn't look too scary.

He didn't reply. He was very weak and had a depleted health bar. He looked over at me and asked, "Can you craft a bed? I'm afraid I might have to respawn and I'd rather respawn here than in the last prison."

I looked through my inventory and luckily I had enough resources to craft a bed for him. As I worked on it, I asked him, "Why are you here?"

"I was treasure hunting in a Nether fortress when a group of people trapped me. They held their swords to me and told me I had to follow them. I didn't want to get destroyed, so I followed them down a hole. They led me to a tiny cell, where they kept me prisoner for a long time, all by myself. I have no idea why they moved me. But this morning, they brought me here. I'm glad for the company."

I finished the bed and the man thanked me. "What's your name?" I asked.

"I'm Sean."

"I'm William."

Sean paused. "You're not William the world-famous explorer . . . are you?"

"I am, actually."

"Oh no. If you're trapped here, that means the people who captured us are extremely powerful. If someone like you can't escape, I'll never make it out of here! You know all the tricks of the Overworld."

I didn't know how to reply. I was both flattered and offended. "I think we will find our way out of here together," I said finally.

"Really? Do you?"

"I hope so. But it's not going to be easy."

"As long as we get out of here," said Sean.

We could hear someone shouting, a muffled voice through the walls. "Do you know if other people are being held prisoner down here?" I asked Sean.

"I'm sure we're not the only ones."

I thought about Oliver. I wondered if he was kept prisoner in one of these cells. I also wondered how many other people were trapped in this prison. If we could get them all to escape, maybe we'd have a better chance of fighting our unknown enemy. The voice grew louder.

Sean walked over to the wall. "I can hear them calling for help!"

"I wish we could help them." I stood beside Sean.

"Me too."

The voices stopped. I wondered if their owners had been destroyed. There was an eerie silence.

"What happened?" Sean put his ear against the wall, hoping to hear something. Anything.

"I don't know. But we will find out," I said.

"Is that a promise?" Sean smiled.

"Yes, it is."

A voice broke through the silence. "Help!"

This time, the voice sounded familiar.

3

IN THE NETHER FORTRESS

wonder where William is trapped. We need to find him as soon as possible. We have to free him and the other prisoners," Harriet said to the group.

Oliver was thinking about the cries that William and Sean had heard. "That wasn't my voice," he said. "I wonder who it was."

"We'll find them." Julian sounded extremely confident.

"How?" asked Harriet, skeptical. The Nether was so big.

"We need to read more of the journal," said Toby.

"We need to find Ezra," Julian reminded them.

"We will find Ezra. But first we need to read the journal."

Julian flipped open the journal again and was about to read from it when an arrow struck him. "Ouch!" he cried and then he dropped the book.

"It's Veronica!" shouted Harriet.

"And Valentino!" Toby cried as he took out his bow and arrow and shot in the direction of the two treasure hunters. They were going to be trouble after all.

The duo ran toward the gang. They put away their bows and arrows and took out enchanted diamond swords. With all their might, they began to attack the group.

"There are only two of you!" Toby shouted at Valentino and Veronica as he fought back with his sword. "You guys will never win."

Then, Valentino called out. "Help!"

At his signal, a group of red men emerged from behind a lava waterfall. They sprinted toward the group. They carried diamond swords and descended upon the gang.

Veronica laughed as she struck Toby. "You guys are never going to win."

"What do you want from us?" asked a terrified Jack.

"We want the book you're reading," Veronica told them. "Give it to us now and you won't get hurt. Otherwise we'll destroy every one of you."

Toby fumbled with his sword as Veronica struck him again. His health bar was dangerously low. Harriet sprinted toward Toby's side and hit Veronica with her diamond sword. "You aren't going to get away with this," she shouted.

"Look at our red army," Veronica laughed. "We have many people working for us. You won't be able to escape the Nether, and you'll never be able to find your friend."

"Don't threaten me." Harriet plunged her sword into Veronica's side.

"Watch out!" Oliver called to Harriet.

A ghast flew through the sky and shot a fireball at Harriet. Thanks to Oliver's warning, she jumped back just in time. The fireball hit Veronica instead. She was instantly destroyed.

"Veronica!" Valentino called out, running to where she had stood.

The ghast shot another fireball. This one hit Valentino, destroying him as well. Harriet hit the next fireball with her fist, obliterating the ghast. The red soldiers fled.

"We're safe!" Jack was relieved. Toby drank a potion of healing and was happy to see his energy restored. Oliver picked up the ghast tears that the ghast had dropped. They would be useful for making potions.

Julian announced, "But William's journal is missing. One of them must have grabbed it during the battle. How are we going to find him without it?"

"We need to find Veronica and Valentino. I'm sure they're the ones who have the journal." Harriet was upset. She had no idea where Veronica and Valentino might have respawned. It was hard enough having to find William, and now they had to hunt for the devious treasure hunters.

"If they have the journal, they might be able to find William before us. And who knows what they would do to him. They will treat him like a treasure to be sold." Oliver was upset.

"There's no use standing around here and worrying. We have to explore the Nether. It's our only hope," Toby informed them.

Harriet took a deep breath. She wanted to go back to the Overworld. She disliked everything about the Nether. But they couldn't give up. She followed the others as they trekked through the red lava-filled landscape. As a zombie pigman walked past her, she avoided making eye contact.

Jack called out, "I see a Nether fortress."

"Yes, I see it too!" Toby ran toward the fortress.

Three yellow blazes flew in front of the fortress and shot fireballs at the gang.

"I don't have any snowballs left," Harriet announced, ducking to avoid one of the fireballs.

Julian handed some to Harriet. "I think we're all running low. So only throw them if you think you can hit one."

Harriet aimed at one of the black-eyed beasts and hit it dead center with the snowball. "I got one of them!"

With one down, the other two were easier. The gang threw snowballs at the remaining blazes until they were destroyed. Oliver went and collected the blaze rods. "I can use these in my potions," he explained.

When he was finished, the group continued on to the fortress.

The fortress was eerily quiet. Julian led them to the secret treasure room. "It looks like the treasure is still here. Everything is intact."

"We need to unearth it." Oliver stood by Julian. "And we have to do it carefully."

Jack slowly and very cautiously approached the treasure, making sure not to set off the trip wire. "There are two chests."

Toby was excited. "Well, let's see what's inside!"

Jack opened the chests. One contained a collection of enchanted books. "These will come in handy when we want to enchant our diamond swords."

As Jack handed out the enchanted books, one for each of them, Harriet opened the second chest. "Emeralds!"

"Wow!" exclaimed Toby.

"Perfect. Now we can use these to trade for other valuable resources," said Julian. They divvied up the emeralds as well. Excited about their newfound treasures, they all started talking about their plans.

"Shh!" Harriet warned them. "I hear voices."

The group stood in silence. They could hear someone talking in the other room. It sounded like Veronica.

Julian peeked into the room and said in a whisper, "It's them—Veronica and Valentino!"

"What are they doing?" asked Harriet quietly.

"They've got William's journal," Julian told the others. "Veronica's reading it out loud. We need to get it from them now before it's too late."

"Shh!" Harriet warned.

The gang went quiet again. They could hear Veronica reading.

Moving closer to the doorway, they listened as Veronica read aloud to Valentino.

4

JOURNAL ENTRY: LAVA LIFE

Day 2: The Hole

"We need to find our way out of here!" Sean said, frustrated.

"I know," I told him. "But we must remain calm. I think I've heard that voice before. I think I know who it belongs to."

"Who?" asked Sean.

"I think it's Thao."

"You mean Charles's sidekick?" Sean was shocked.

"Yes, but I don't think he is working with Charles anymore. I think he's another prisoner here."

"Why would he be a prisoner?" Sean didn't understand.

"I'm not sure, but that is almost certainly his voice. I think we need to find out why he's here. But first, we need to escape. Time to make a plan. My inventory is empty—what about yours?"

Sean looked through his inventory and took out a pickaxe. "Would this help us?"

"Yes!" I exclaimed. I couldn't believe that Sean had a pickaxe. I was ecstatic. I grabbed the pickaxe and began to dig a hole in the middle of our small cell.

"Stop," Sean told me. "I think I hear something."

The small hole in the wall opened again and another carrot was tossed into the room.

"Food," Sean exclaimed, taking a big bite of the carrot he'd retrieved from the floor. He handed it to me when he'd eaten half of it.

I ate quickly, eager to get back to digging. I wanted to escape so badly.

"Look out!" Sean cried. Before I'd even finished the carrot, a magma cube spawned in our little room. Sean grabbed a sword from his inventory and struck at the cube. It broke into smaller cubes. I wanted to help him, but I didn't have anything in my inventory and felt very helpless. I was impressed with how many items Sean had in his inventory.

"Do you have an extra sword?" I shouted to Sean.

"Yes!" He stopped fighting for a moment and handed it to me. "Keep it."

More magma cubes spawned around us. I had a newfound confidence as I struck one of the magma cubes with the sword. Now that I had a replenished inventory, I could battle alongside Sean. It was also nice to have a partner in this.

"More are spawning!" Sean shouted.

"Don't give up," I cried as I struck another magma cube and it broke into smaller cubes. Sean and I had barely enough energy to fight the bouncy Nether mobs.

When the final cube was destroyed, we sat down, desperately needing a break. We sat there a moment in silence, until Sean asked, "Are you going to keep digging the hole?"

"Yes," I replied. I got up and dug the pickaxe back into the ground.

Sean took a shovel out of his inventory and joined me. Between the pickaxe and the shovel, we made a lot of progress.

I looked down at the hole. "Oh no."

Sean stared at the lava that flowed underneath the floor of our cell.

"Now we'll never escape." I watched the hot lava flow by in despair.

"Help!" a voice called out.

Sean sprinted to the wall. "Can you hear us?"

The voice replied, "Yes! I'm being attacked by magma cubes! Can someone help me?"

Sean grabbed the pickaxe and banged it against the side of the wall, making a small hole. He crawled through the hole and I followed.

When we entered the second cell, we saw a girl with pink hair fighting three magma cubes all by herself. She was very low on energy and she was using all the energy she had to battle the mobs.

I struck a cube with my sword and Sean destroyed the smaller cubes. Within the three of us working together, the magma cubes were quickly taken care of.

"Thank you so much!" the girl with pink hair said to us.

"Who are you?" I asked.

"My name is Molly," she replied and then quickly added, "You guys better leave. If they find you in here, they will destroy us all. I've heard that they set some prisoners to Hardcore mode and destroy them for good."

"Seriously?" Sean was shocked.

"Yes," said Molly. "I've been here a long time. I've seen some pretty awful things. I used to have a cellmate, but she disappeared. I don't know what happened to her, but I never saw her again." Molly began to cry.

"Who was your cellmate?" asked Sean. "We can help you find her."

"Her name was Esther. But it's been a long time since I last saw her. I doubt we'll find her. Sometimes I imagine her safe and happy in the Overworld. And anyway, we're stuck in here."

"Molly,"—I really meant this when I said it—"we're going to get out of here. I know it."

"How?" she asked.

"Well, we tried digging down, but there's lava running below us. We need to come up with a new plan. Luckily Sean still has a pretty well-stocked inventory, so that should help. Do you happen to have any resources we can use?"

"I don't have much—just a couple of potions and a bucket."

"A bucket," I thought aloud, "that might come in handy. If we put some of the lava in the bucket, we can use it to attack the person who is bringing us the food."

"Why would we want to do that? We need that food to survive," said Molly.

"We need to escape," I replied. "This could help us do that."

"I've been here so long, I don't want to escape. I'd be too afraid to leave," she confessed.

"We are going to escape. Of course it won't be easy, but nothing important ever is."

Molly thought about those words. She went through her inventory and pulled out a potion of invisibility. "Do you think this could help?"

I smiled. "Absolutely."

Molly followed us back to our cell. I had a million plans racing through my mind. I had to pick the perfect one. Of course, I knew they were all risky.

"What do we do next?" asked Sean.

"We're going to knock down this wall." I pointed to the wall that had the small hole where the unknown person dropped our daily carrot ration.

They didn't ask any further questions. We each grabbed a tool and attacked the wall together.

5
THE TREASURE HUNTERS

C an you hear them?" whispered Harriet.
"They stopped reading." Julian peeked into the
other room again.

Valentino lunged at Julian as he turned the corner,
striking him with a diamond sword. "It's over!"

Julian grabbed his own diamond sword and battled
Valentino.

Toby sprinted toward Veronica and splashed a potion
of harming on her, then tried to grab the journal.

Then three blazes spawned in the room. They unleash-
ed a sea of fireballs at the group. One of the fireballs
struck Oliver, destroying him.

"Oliver!" Julian cried. "Now he'll respawn in the desert! Oh no!"

The group had very few snowballs left, which made
the battle against the blazes almost impossible.

Julian struck Valentino with his diamond sword as
they both tried to avoid the fiery blasts.

Harriet shielded herself from the fireballs, but it was too late. There was no escape. She was hit by one of the fireballs and she too was destroyed.

"Harriet's gone, too!" Jack called out as he helped Julian destroy Valentino with his sword.

Veronica was devastated when she saw her partner destroyed, and she didn't notice the fireball that was headed in her direction. She was almost instantly destroyed as well.

No longer distracted, the remaining gang fought desperately until the final blaze was defeated. Toby collected the blaze rods to give to Oliver, hoping they would see him again soon.

"What are we going to do?" asked Jack. "Oliver and Harriet will have both respawned in the desert. Should we go back for them?"

Everyone had a different opinion. Toby wanted to find Harriet first. Julian was still worried about Ezra. "At least we know that Oliver and Harriet are okay. Charles has Ezra, and we still don't know if William is safe. They should be our priority."

"I think we have to go back to the Overworld, even if Harriet and Oliver aren't in as much danger," said Jack. "We have no snowballs left in our inventories. If we have one more attack from a fiery Nether mob, we will all be destroyed. We need to restock our inventories and find our friends."

Julian nodded his head slowly. "Maybe you're right."

"Let's make a portal back to the Overworld," said Toby.

The group left the Nether fortress and headed toward the lava waterfall where they could craft a portal.

"Look!" Toby called out. "I see a bucket."

Toby walked over to a bucket that was on the netherrack ground. He picked it up and handed it to Julian.

"Who would have left this here?" asked Julian.

Jack thought about the journal. "Oh!" he exclaimed. "Do you think this bucket could be a clue?"

"A clue?" asked Julian.

"Yes, to finding William," said Jack.

"It could be Molly's bucket!" said Toby.

"It could be anybody's bucket," said Julian.

"Okay, it doesn't matter who the bucket belongs to. For now we need to get back to the Overworld." Jack was annoyed.

"All right, all right," said Julian. "We're making the portal. Happy?"

"Yes," replied Jack. But before they activated the portal, the group heard a voice call out to them.

"Help me! Don't leave me here!" the voice shouted.

"It sounds like Ezra! We need to find him," said Julian.

Toby was ready to activate the portal. "But the portal is complete. We have to travel back to the Overworld."

"I can't leave now. I'm certain that was Ezra calling for us. Let's just leave the portal and come back," insisted Julian.

"What if this is a trick?" asked Jack.

"There's only one way to find out," said Julian. Jack and Toby gave in. They would have done the same if the roles were reversed, if they had heard Harriet calling for help.

The group followed Julian toward the cries. They were walking up a series of steps leading to a bridge that crossed a large lava river when Julian called out, "I see him!"

Ezra was on the bridge. Valentino and Veronica had him cornered. They had their swords pointed at him, and his energy bar was very low. With one hit from a diamond sword, he'd be destroyed.

Toby took out his bow and arrow and aimed at Valentino. He struck him on his first shot. Valentino turned around and ran toward Toby, ready for a fight.

Ezra was able to break free from Veronica and he too began to run toward Toby.

Then a loud roar interrupted them. Everybody stopped where they were.

"Is that the—" Julian looked up in disbelief.

"It can't be!" cried Valentino.

The Ender Dragon flew through the red Nether sky. Someone had summoned the beast from the End and brought it to the Nether.

One of the dragon's scaly wings struck Veronica, throwing her off the bridge and into the lava river. Valentino cried out. But he didn't have time to mourn his partner, because the dragon was coming right for him next. In a matter of seconds, the dragon had thrown Valentino from the bridge as well.

"Get to the portal!" Toby called to his friends. "I'm going to ignite it!" The gang sprinted as fast as they could. Ezra had barely enough energy to keep up.

A purple mist rose up as they stepped onto the portal and back to the Overworld.

The portal left them in a grassy area of the Overworld.

"We need to find the desert," said Jack.

But the sun was beginning to set. The group crafted a crudely constructed house to spend the night in. As they crawled into their beds, Julian remembered that he had retrieved the journal when he was battling Valentino and Veronica. "I have the book. Should I read from it?"

"Yes," replied Toby and Jack in unison.

Julian began to read.

6

JOURNAL ENTRY: HOPEFUL ESCAPE

Day 3: Crumbling Wall

As we worked on knocking down the wall, Sean suddenly went still and whispered, "Stop. I hear something."

A head looked through the hole. "What are you doing?" a voice growled.

We were frozen in fear. Before we could respond, three blazes spawned in the center of the room and blew fireballs in our direction.

Molly threw a snowball at one of the blazes, destroying the yellow beast. But I did nothing. I tried to escape the flames, but I couldn't. I was destroyed. Again.

I respawned in the prison cell and awoke to Sean defeating the final blaze. Can you blame me for fearing fire? It had destroyed me so many times. I sprinted toward the wall and peeked through the hole. "There's nobody out there."

"They must have spawned blazes in the cell to punish us," said Molly. She started collecting the blaze rods. "But these will come in handy."

Before we could even catch our breaths, a group of magma cubes spawned in the cell and bounced toward us. Sean took out his sword and lunged at the cubes. "You're right," he said, "I bet they're going to keep summoning hostile mobs."

I used the pickaxe to help battle the bouncy creatures. "How are we going to go on like this? I don't want to be destroyed twice in one day. This is worse than just being trapped in here. What if they don't stop?"

"Then we're in trouble!" shouted Molly as she destroyed a magma cube.

"What are we going to do?" Sean asked, fighting to destroy the smaller cubes as they spread out.

"Watch out!" I called to Sean. He was getting close to the hole in the ground. I didn't want him to fall in and be destroyed by the lava.

"Thanks!" he replied breathlessly, still battling the fiery mobs.

"This is awful." Molly was exhausted, battling the remaining cube. "What's our plan?"

"We're going to escape," I said. I wanted to convince myself that this was possible. I had my doubts, but I knew it was the only way we could survive. I also wanted to find Thao. Now that he was Charles's enemy, he might be a helpful ally.

The battle was intense, but we destroyed the final magma cube. I held on to my pickaxe and began to chip at the wall again.

"We can't do that!" Molly warned me. "It will draw attention to us and they will just have more hostile mobs spawn here. We need to do something that they can't hear or see. We have to appear to be model prisoners and when they aren't looking we can plan an escape."

Molly was right. Her idea sounded smart, but I didn't know how we could escape without bringing attention to ourselves.

"What should we do?" I asked her.

"I think we should go back into my room and try digging a hole in the ground. We don't know that there is a stream of lava running beneath my room too," she said. With that, she crawled through the hole back into her cell.

We followed Molly and began to dig.

"I don't see any lava yet, do you?" I asked.

"Nope," replied Sean.

We dug for awhile, and we still hadn't hit any lava. Sean crawled through the hole and began to search for a way out.

"I see light!" he called out.

"Should we climb in?" I asked.

"Yes," Sean replied. "We can dig from below."

Molly and I climbed into the hole, and together we dug a tunnel to the outside. We emerged by a lava stream. Molly held her bucket in one hand. She had filled it and was ready to throw lava on any enemy.

I took my first steps outside of the prison. Although I disliked the Nether, I was so happy to be free.

"I can't believe we did it. We escaped!" Molly was filled with glee.

"I know. The plan worked." The minute those words fell from my lips, a group of ghasts flew through the sky, aiming their fireballs at us.

"What are we going to do?" Sean asked nervously.

"Does anyone have a bow and arrow?" I asked them.

"No," Molly and Sean responded together.

"We can hit the fireballs with our fists and send them back to the ghasts," I said. We were running low on resources and we had no weapons to fight back with. We were going to have to make do.

Molly took out the potion of invisibility and splashed us. "This might be easier."

"That sounds like an even better plan," I said.

Although we couldn't see each other, we tried to stick together as we sprinted away from the ghasts.

"I see a Nether fortress," Molly called out to us.

"Me too!"

We ran toward the fortress. Once we were inside, the potion wore off and we were visible again.

"Let's hunt for treasure," Sean said.

We should have been crafting a portal back to the Overworld, but when Sean suggested that we search for treasure, we all agreed with him. It was too tempting to resist in a Nether fortress.

We entered the room where the treasure was stored and began to unearth the chests. Sean opened the first chest.

"Diamonds!" he called out.

"What a find!" Molly doled out the diamonds to each of us and we placed them in our inventories.

I opened the second chest. "It's filled with enchanted books."

We quickly added the enchanted books to our inventories too. Then Molly searched the fortress for other resources. She found Nether wart, which she gathered up carefully. "This will help me brew potions."

I looked over at her. "Where's your bucket?"

Molly checked her inventory. "I must have dropped it by the lava stream."

"Should we go back and get it?" I asked.

Sean and Molly paused and I could see that they weren't sure if that was a good idea. Sean replied, "I think we should craft a portal to the Overworld. Forget the bucket."

We all agreed that was a good plan. We left the Nether fortress and began to craft a portal. As we finished building it, an arrow struck me. I looked up in surprise. A voice called out, "Where do you think you're going?"

7
SIDETRACKED

So the bucket did belong to them." Toby was excited. They had a clue and they were a little closer to finding William and his friends.

"That could have been Molly's bucket," said Jack, "but we aren't even in the Nether anymore. We have to find Harriet and Oliver and get back there. Even if we were right near them it doesn't matter, because we are far from them now."

Everyone agreed—they had to find Harriet and Oliver quickly and then get back to the Nether. But now it was time to sleep. They drifted off one by one, and the group dreamt about finding their lost friends and finally meeting William the Explorer. Toby dreamt of the parties they would attend in the Overworld, once they reintroduced the world to its lost explorer. The people of the Overworld would be overjoyed to see William.

When the sun came up, Jack walked outside in search of something to eat. He spotted a chicken in the distance.

With his bow and arrow, he destroyed the chicken. He retrieved it and then went back into the house and offered the others some food.

"We need to fill up our food bars, before we embark on this journey," he said, handing each person some chicken.

The group devoured the chicken as they plotted their path to the desert. Toby asked, "Do you think that Harriet and Oliver are still there?"

"Yes," said Jack. "That's where they will have respawned and they'll stay there because they'll know we're looking for them."

The group made their way to the desert. Ezra suggested, "I know this is a bit out of the way, but I think we should take a detour to the cold biome and replenish our supply of snowballs."

Everyone wanted to get to Harriet and Oliver quickly, but they realized this was a good plan. It would all be for nothing if they returned to the Nether without snowballs.

Jack looked at the map and led the group up a mountain and toward the cold biome. As they climbed the mountain, Julian looked out into the distance and spotted his town. He missed his wheat farm and the comforts of home. He imagined returning to the town with William and Oliver. He remembered the last time they had visited his town. William's fame had transformed him and he had acted like a different person entirely. Julian had been very upset with him. Julian hoped that when he found William, he would be more like the old William he had known.

As they made their way down the mountain on the other side, Julian noticed the piles of snow. Just what they needed.

The group ran toward the snow and began to craft as many snowballs as they could fit in their inventories.

"I think we have enough," said Toby after a while.

"Yes, and now we really need to head to the desert," said Jack.

The group climbed back up the mountain. Julian stopped again to look out at his town. It made him happy to think about home, and that was something he wanted to share. "I can see my town from the top of the mountain," he told the others.

"When this journey is over," Jack promised Julian, "we will all go back to your town to celebrate."

"I'd like that." Julian smiled.

The trip to the desert was long, and the sun was beginning to set. The group had to construct another house to spend the night in. They didn't want to battle the hostile mobs that spawned in the middle of the night.

They picked a patch of grass in the middle of the jungle and began to construct the house. As they were building it, Ezra spotted a jungle temple. "In the morning we should go to that temple and search for treasure."

"We don't have time. We already lost valuable time getting snowballs. We don't want to keep getting sidetracked," argued Jack.

The others didn't agree. Julian said, "I think we need to fill our inventories with as many resources as we can.

We don't know when we'll be back. We can't pass up searching for treasure in the jungle temple."

They all climbed into bed. When they woke up, they dressed in their diamond armor, and prepared to travel to the jungle temple. They made their way through the jungle in hopes of finding a trove of useful treasure.

They entered the grand temple and headed to the room with the treasure. When they reached the treasure room, they spotted two people wearing sparkly purple helmets. They were already there trying to unearth the treasure.

Toby shot an arrow at them.

"What are you doing?" hissed Jack.

"I want the treasure," said Toby, unapologetically.

"But they got to it first. Let's just go. This isn't how we behave." Jack was upset. Things weren't the same without Harriet around.

The others agreed with Jack. Julian said, "We'll find other treasures. These people have discovered the treasure before us, and it's rightfully theirs."

But it was too late. The two people in the sparkly purple helmets turned around and began to shoot arrows at the gang.

"See what you did?" Jack shouted at Toby.

"I'm sorry," Toby said to his friends and then called out to the purple helmets, "Please. Stop. We surrender."

The purple-helmeted duo approached the gang. "What do you want from us?"

Toby replied, "We are going to leave."

"Not so fast," said one of the purple-helmeted people.

"Please, we have somewhere we need to be," Jack tried to explain.

"You attacked us," said the purple-helmeted treasure hunter.

The gang knew it wasn't going to be an easy escape. They had attacked these people and now they were going to pay the price. Jack was very upset. He didn't want them to get sidetracked and now they were about to be in a completely unnecessary battle with these two strangers.

"Please, just be happy with your treasure and let us go on our way," Toby tried to reason with them.

One of the purple-helmeted people took out a bow and arrow.

Toby grabbed a potion of invisibility and splashed it on his friends. They sprinted out of the temple.

When the potion wore off and they reappeared, they were in the desert. "That was a close call," said Julian.

Then Toby spotted Harriet in the distance. "Harriet!" he called out.

She ran toward him. "What are you guys doing here? I thought you'd still be in the Nether."

"We came to get you and Oliver," Toby told her.

"I don't know where Oliver is. I haven't seen him at all," Harriet told her friends.

"Well, we have to find him," Jack told the group.

Before the group could enjoy their reunion and strategize about finding Oliver, Veronica and Valentino appeared in front of them.

"How did you get here?" asked Julian, caught by surprise.

"We TPed," replied Veronica. "Now give us the journal."

"No. Never!" shouted Julian.

Valentino struck Julian with his sword. "If you don't give it to us, then you better start reading from it."

The gang didn't want to give the journal away. They also didn't want to fight again. So Julian read.

8
JOURNAL ENTRY:
A NEW FRIEND

Day 4: Portal

Nobody spoke.

The voice called out again. "I said, where do you think you're going?"

Molly replied, "We are going to the Overworld. Ignite the portal, William."

Before I could ignite the portal, I was hit by a sea of arrows and destroyed. I respawned in the prison cell. I waited for Sean to respawn in the room, but he didn't. I hoped Sean and Molly had made it to the Overworld, but I was also sad that I was alone. I looked through my inventory and pulled out the pickaxe. I crawled through the hole and into Molly's room. I jumped into the hole we had dug and ran down the dark tunnel toward my friends.

I emerged back in the Nether and sprinted in the direction of the portal. I watched as two men dressed in black destroyed Sean and Molly. Instead of going through the portal by myself, I went back to the hole. I wanted to be reunited with my new friends and come up with another plan of escape. We would be stronger together. When I crawled back into the room, Molly was respawning. She looked over at me.

"Who was the person who destroyed us?" she asked me.

"I think it was Charles. He was dressed in black, so I'm not certain, but if it wasn't him, I'm sure it was somebody that works for him."

Sean appeared too. "Guys, we have to get back to the portal. We need to get back to the Overworld."

"I know, but now they know where we constructed the portal and it's too dangerous to return to that spot," I said. "They're obviously stronger than we are, even working as a team."

"I guess we'll have to craft another portal," suggested Molly.

We could hear a cry for help from the other room. Molly ran to the wall, "Oh!" she cried out. "That sounds like my old cellmate!" She called out, "Esther is that you?"

"Molly! Yes, it's me. Please help me."

"We have to break down this wall, fast." Molly pulled her pickaxe out of her inventory.

Sean began to bang a hole in the wall. "I think I see something."

We joined in and helped break down the wall. I climbed through the hole, but was instantly destroyed when a blaze shot a fireball at me. When I respawned, there were three people standing by me. I recognized Molly and Sean, but didn't know the third person.

"Thanks for trying to help me. I'm Esther," she introduced herself.

"Hi. Molly told us about you."

"Molly told me how you guys are going to escape," she said. "I tried to escape before and it was awful. I was alone in the Nether. I finally was about to make it back to the Overworld when Charles trapped me again."

"What about Thao? I thought I heard him cry for help. Is he being kept prisoner down here?" I asked.

"Yes, Thao and Charles aren't working together anymore."

"So what's the plan?" Molly asked us. "How are we going to escape this time?"

"We're going to crawl through the tunnel we made and try to escape in another direction of the Nether," I suggested. "Do you still have any bottles left of the potion of invisibility?"

Molly checked her inventory. "Yes. One bottle left."

"That's good to know," I said, "but we should only use that when we are in real trouble. I'd rather respawn here and start over than use it up—agreed?"

They agreed and we each jumped into the tunnel and started our journey to freedom again. When we climbed out of the hole, there was Charles, standing right in front of us.

"You think you can escape?" he asked with a sinister laugh. It had been his voice I'd heard through the wall.

"Yes," I replied confidently.

Sean took out his diamond sword and struck Charles.

Charles grabbed his own sword and fought back, laughing, "You think you can battle me and win?"

"Yes." Sean struck Charles again.

This angered Charles. "Well, you won't. I have you trapped. Just like I have your friend Oliver trapped in the desert."

"Oliver? Where?" I was so happy to just hear his name. We had to save him.

"Where is Oliver? Where are your weapons?" Charles laughed even louder. "You can't even battle me, can you? I bet you don't feel like such a brave world explorer now."

He thought I didn't have a weapon, so I couldn't join in the battle. But I had a diamond sword. I took it out and lunged toward Charles. Molly and Esther joined in the fight. I actually thought we had a chance, but the minute he seemed to weaken, Charles laughed even harder. He had backup, and he ordered a bunch of men dressed in black to shoot. A barrage of arrows hit us and we respawned in our rooms.

I looked over at Sean. "What are we going to do? Now we can't even travel through the tunnel."

Sean looked up at the ceiling. "I think I have a new plan."

9
TREASURE TROVE

Keep reading!" Veronica shouted at Julian.

"That's it. There isn't anything else. It looks like some pages were ripped out. Or maybe he started another journal." He showed her the book.

"You are trying to trick us." Veronica was angry and she struck him with her diamond sword.

"No, see for yourself. There aren't any other pages." Julian showed Veronica the book again.

Veronica was annoyed. "We have to get those missing pages. I am going to find William. I am going to get credit for discovering the world-famous explorer."

"We want to find William because we want him to be free. We aren't doing it so everyone in the Overworld will respect and look up to us. We are doing it for him." Julian looked at Veronica.

"Semantics. We all want to find him. And I will be first." She smiled and ran off to join Valentino.

Harriet watched them take off. "Do you think they'll find the missing pages before we do?"

Julian replied, "I don't know. But we'd better start looking."

"Where should we start?" asked Harriet.

Julian said, "I think we should really spend our time searching for Oliver first. And then we need to make our way back to the Nether."

Everyone agreed. They walked through the desert, hoping they would find Oliver. They called his name aloud, but there was no response.

"Do you think he is being kept prisoner?" asked Harriet.

"You're right!" Julian's face lit up. "He probably respawned in the stronghold underneath the desert temple and can't escape."

The gang ran toward the desert temple. Toby spotted the hole in the ground. "This is the entrance to the stronghold where Oliver was kept prisoner before."

The group entered the stronghold. The first room was infested with silverfish. They took out their diamond swords and began to destroy the small insects. Although the pesky creatures weren't as harmful as other mobs, the sheer number of silverfish that blanketed the floor of the main room in the stronghold was overpowering.

Jack called out, "We need to find the spawner and deactivate it!"

"Yes, I'll try and find it," called Harriet. "Keep fighting!" She sprinted deeper into the stronghold in search of the spawner. She found it in a small room off the main hallway and called for help.

Jack sprinted toward Harriet and helped her deactivate the spawner.

They raced back to their friends and helped destroy the remaining silverfish. The gang explored the rest of the stronghold, searching for the room where Oliver had been kept prisoner.

"Oliver!" Julian called out.

"Ouch!" Toby cried. "I've been struck by an arrow."

Harriet looked ahead and yelled, "Skeletons!"

A small group of skeletons approached the group. Everyone took out their weapons, but they were all very low on energy and had to win this battle fast or they would be destroyed. It was a dangerous battle. Julian struck one of the bony beasts with his diamond sword, destroying it. The skeleton dropped a bone and Julian quickly picked it up and placed it in his inventory.

Jack battled two skeletons with his diamond sword and he skillfully obliterated both of them. They dropped bones, which he collected.

"We did it! We destroyed the skeletons!" Harriet was excited for their victory.

"I'm worried that our energy levels are getting too low," Julian said as he handed potions of strength to the gang. "Drink these to regain your strength."

The group drank the potions. As Harriet finished, she looked down on the ground. "What's that?" she asked as she leaned over to pick up pages off the floor.

Julian stood next to Harriet. "I think those are the missing pages from the journal."

Harriet asked, "How did they get here?" She leafed through the pages and confirmed, "These are definitely the missing pages."

"However they got here, we have to read them," said Toby.

"No, we need to find Oliver first. I don't like being in this stronghold. It makes us vulnerable. Charles could trap us down here," Julian argued, walking deeper into the stronghold before anyone could stop him.

Harriet hesitated. "I think I hear something."

"Me too," said Ezra. "It sounds like it's coming from behind that wall."

A muffled voice called out, "Is someone there? Help me!"

"It sounds like Oliver!" Julian sprinted toward the sound of the voice.

As the voice grew louder, the group became more hopeful. They wanted to find their friend Oliver and free him from the stronghold.

"It sounds like he is trapped over here." Julian ran to a wall and took out his pickaxe. He banged against the wall.

"I see a hole!" Oliver called out. "Is that you, Julian?"

"It's me!" he shouted back. "We'll save you—don't worry! It will only take a few minutes."

A loud laugh boomed through the stronghold. "You think I'm going to let him escape me twice?" It was Charles. He stood behind the group, and pointed his diamond sword at them.

"You can't trap Oliver. We are going to free him and find William. Your reign of terror is over," Julian shouted at the villain.

"What a nice plan. If only you could actually follow through with it. You are all now my prisoners." He called to a group of soldiers dressed in black, "Get them!"

The soldiers sprinted toward the gang and began to strike them with their diamond swords.

"Stop!" Charles ordered the soldiers. "Take them to their new home." He let out another loud sinister laugh.

The group was defeated. Julian asked, "Can't we stay with Oliver?"

"No, he will stay alone in his prison. You will be kept separate from him. Enjoy your life in a prison cell." Charles's laugh grew deeper.

The gang was led into a small room lined with beds. The soldiers closed the door behind them. Almost immediately, a silverfish spawned in the center of the room. Julian hit the insect with his diamond sword.

"What are we going to do?" asked Toby.

The group could hear Oliver crying for help and they felt powerless. They were all upset that they were being kept prisoner and were losing hope quickly. Harriet took the missing journal pages from her inventory and said, "We're going to read."

10
JOURNAL ENTRY: SMALL EXPLORATION

Day 5: Going Up

"I think we can try to dig our way out from the top," said Sean.

    This seemed like a good plan, but it also appeared to be quite difficult to pull off. I didn't know how we'd reach the ceiling. We didn't have a ladder and it was very high up. And once we reached the top, we might not be able to actually escape. It wouldn't take us very far and Charles would probably spot us and force us back to the prison. Again. I told this to Sean and his face grew very sad. "I'm sorry. It seemed like a good idea, but you're right—I don't think it will work. I'm trying to come up with a plan that would work. I want to get out of here." He was upset.

    "We all want to get out of here, and we will," I reassured him. "Now we have both Molly and Esther helping us. I think the more people we have on our side, the better. There is strength in numbers and we are going to need all the resources we can gather to battle Charles."

"You're right," Sean said. He went over to the hole in the wall and asked Molly and Esther if we could join them in their cell. We were going to strategize yet another plan of escape.

Molly and Esther had some ideas of their own. They wanted to make a hole in Esther's wall and free the person who lived in the next cell over.

"There is a voice that calls for help all the time," said Esther. "And the more people we have on our side, the more likely we'll be able to fight back."

"I think it's Thao," I commented. "We should try to get to him. He was Charles's partner. He could be incredibly helpful, because he knows Charles better than we do."

We climbed through the hole in the wall to reach Esther's room. I stood by the opposite wall and spoke. "Who are you?"

The voice was weak. "I need help. I am trapped here and I have been attacked by hostile mobs every day. I have no energy and all they feed me is a carrot per day."

"This is happening to all of us. But if you want me to help you, you must tell me who you are," I said.

"I don't see how that is important." The voice sounded even weaker. "I just need help. Can you help me?"

Before I could respond, two blazes spawned in Esther's room. She quickly grabbed a snowball from her inventory and threw it at the yellow beast, but a fireball struck me and I was destroyed.

I respawned in my bed. My friends were by my side. "Are the blazes destroyed?" I asked.

"Yes." Esther smiled. "And we have someone we want to introduce you to."

Then Thao walked into the room.

My heart skipped a beat. Although I knew he wasn't working with Charles any longer, I still remembered the many battles I had fought against him. It was going to be hard to work with someone I had considered my enemy, someone who had destroyed my life, who had destroyed my best friend's life. But he was also a fellow prisoner, and now we had a common goal. We both wanted to escape.

"I know who you are," I replied finally.

"I'm sorry for all the trouble I have caused you in the past. Esther set me free and now I want to work with you guys to escape from this prison. I'm no longer working with Charles. He turned against me. I can't trust him anymore."

I listened to Thao talk about Charles. I wanted to believe that he could have changed and that he was truly on our side this time, but I was wary. I knew how mean he could be and it was hard to let that go. "I'm going to accept your apology, but I want you to know that you were very destructive when I was an explorer. Both you and Charles tried to stop me from sharing my discoveries with the Overworld. I'm not sure I can trust you."

"I was being forced to do that because of Charles," he replied.

"You don't have to do things just because others want you to do them. You're responsible for your own decisions."

"I promise that even once we are free and back in the Overworld, I will think for myself and will only help others."

Thao sounded sincere. And I knew it would be helpful to have him on our side.

"Is there anything that you know about Charles that would help us? You worked with him for so long—you must know some of his secret plans and his weaknesses."

Thao paused and thought for a moment. "I know a lot about this space. I was here when Charles built it. If we get to the room next to yours, there is a tunnel to a stronghold and we can escape through there."

"Excellent!" I replied. We took out our tools and chipped away at the wall until it began to crumble.

Peeking through the hole we'd made, Esther said, "I think I can fit through now." She crawled through first.

I kept banging the wall with my pickaxe to create a larger hole. "Esther, what's in there?"

"It's empty. But Thao is right—there is a hole in the ground and it looks like it leads to a tunnel."

"Great," I said. "Wait for us. We'll be there in a minute."

We finally made a gaping hole in the wall big enough for all of us to climb through. We followed Esther down the hole, into the ground.

Molly was nervous as we entered the long tunnel to the stronghold. "What if this is a trap?"

Thao reassured her. "I know how to escape from this stronghold. We just have to avoid Charles. So we need to be very quiet."

We silently made our way into the stronghold as we followed Thao. I hoped he couldn't hear my heart—it was beating very fast and very loud.

11
BATTLE IN THE NETHER

We are all trapped in a stronghold," Jack pointed out. "What a coincidence."

"Well," said Julian, "it looks like reading isn't going to help us here. We need to escape, free Oliver, and get back to the Nether. We can't waste any more time."

Harriet put the pages back in her inventory and began to pace in the small room.

"How?" Toby asked.

"We are going to break down this wall." Julian took out his pickaxe and banged into the wall. As the wall crumbled, the others joined him.

"I hope Charles doesn't catch us," Toby said as he banged his own pickaxe against the wall.

"And what about his army?" Jack was worried but he also wanted to escape.

"We have no choice. We need to escape this room." Julian finished a large hole in the wall and the group

57

crawled through. They ran toward the room where Oliver was being kept prisoner.

Harriet heard a noise. "*Guys, stop!*" She called to her friends in a loud whisper. "Take this." She handed them a potion of invisibility and the group drank it and disappeared.

They walked up to Oliver's room. Julian called out quietly, "*Oliver*, we are breaking down the wall."

Harriet kept watch. Even though they were invisible, the soldiers that guarded the prison would be able to see the pickaxe.

Julian made a large hole and Oliver crawled through. Before they could celebrate the reunion, Harriet splashed a potion of invisibility on Oliver and together they sprinted out of the stronghold and through the desert. As they reached the jungle, the potion wore off.

Jack looked at the others. "Finally, we're all together again." He was relieved. He'd been worried that one of them might have gotten lost when they were invisible.

"We need to craft a portal to the Nether," Toby said.

They all agreed and began to craft a portal. They climbed into the portal and a purple mist rose up around them. In the distance they could see Charles and his army sprinting toward them, but it was too late. They had truly escaped. Once they arrived in the red landscape of the Nether, Jack broke the portal.

"We don't want Charles following us here," he said.

The gang filled Oliver in on what had happened in the last journal entry. "We know they were trapped in a stronghold," Harriet informed him.

"But where?" asked Oliver.

"We aren't sure, but we'll find out," said Ezra.

"Maybe we should stop and read a little more. It might help us find the stronghold," suggested Oliver.

"Actually," said Harriet, "we don't have anything left to read. There were a bunch of pages missing from the journal. We found a few of them, but the others are still missing."

"Do we have any idea where they could be?" asked Oliver.

"We don't know," said Ezra. "But we do know that Veronica and Valentino are also searching for the missing pages and for William."

"Wow," exclaimed Oliver. "We have a lot to do."

"Yes," said Julian, "but we have clues. We need to go back to the spot where we saw Molly's bucket. The stronghold isn't far from there."

"We should be on the lookout for Veronica and Valentino over there. They know about that clue, too," added Jack.

The group made their way through the Nether and toward the lava stream where they had found Molly's bucket.

"Here we are," Harriet said as she looked down at the stream. "We should start looking for holes in the ground."

Three blazes flew through the sky. But the gang was prepared this time. They gathered the snowballs they had collected and threw them at the yellow fiery mobs, annihilating them quickly.

"I see a hole!" Harriet called out.

The group was running toward Harriet when Oliver called out, "Ouch!"

An arrow had hit him, and now Veronica and Valentino raced toward them. "You aren't going down that hole. We are!"

Valentino splashed a potion of weakness on the group and suddenly they were frozen in place. They couldn't move as their hearts depleted. The group watched as Veronica and Valentino climbed into the hole in search of William.

"We need to follow them," Julian called out when he could speak again.

Before they had a chance to take his advice, they heard Veronica and Valentino scream and then saw them sprint from the hole.

"What happened?" Harriet asked.

"It's filled with lava. You guys were trying to trick us. Admit it, the journal is a hoax." Veronica aimed her sword at Harriet.

"No. But why would the hole be filled with lava?" asked Ezra.

Nobody wanted to say it, but everyone was worried that William and his friends had been destroyed by lava. Charles might have flooded the stronghold to destroy them. Oliver's face collapsed. They all stood by the hole and stared.

"Where is the rest of the journal?" Valentino pointed his sword at the gang. "We need to know where William is being kept prisoner."

"Maybe this was the place and now he is destroyed," Jack said glumly.

"I don't believe you." Valentino struck Jack with his sword. Jack was too weak to fight back and feared that he'd respawn in the Overworld.

They were saved by a group of ghasts. The ghasts flew toward them, and Valentino was hit by a fireball and destroyed. Jack was relieved. He had enough strength to hit one of the blasts with his fist and destroy the ghast. Veronica, unable to fight the group as well as the ghasts, was soon also struck by a fireball and destroyed. The group began to regain their energy and fought the ghasts with their fists. They were happy when the final ghast was destroyed. Oliver made sure to gather up the dropped gunpowder.

Julian looked down on the ground. "No way!" he called out.

"What?" asked Ezra.

"I think I found pages from the journal." Julian picked them up and inspected them. "They are the missing pages!"

"Read them!" Harriet called out.

Julian paused and asked the group, "Do you think this is a trap? Do you think Valentino and Veronica are trying to trick us? I mean they leave and we find the journal pages. It just seems a little suspicious."

The group agreed, but Harriet said, "Maybe we should read them and see what we think. It could be that they had these pages and they just dropped them. We can't be sure that they are tricking us."

The group kept a close watch for hostile mobs as Julian read aloud from William's journal.

12
JOURNAL ENTRY: FALSE START

Day 6: Escape

I was very nervous as we traveled through the tunnel. I wanted to trust Thao. I wanted to believe that we'd be safe, but I was worried and doubtful. When we emerged out into the Nether, I felt much better. I knew that we had to trust Thao, that he also wanted to get back to the Overworld. The further we traveled from the stronghold, the more hopeful I became. I imagined being reunited with my friends and enjoying my life in the Overworld. These were the thoughts that filled my mind, when we spotted three Ender Dragons flying toward us.

Thao asked, "Does anyone have any snowballs?"

I didn't. But Esther had a few. She handed them out and said, "Charles must have summoned these Ender Dragons. He knows we escaped."

We used all of our strength to battle the deadly mobs. Luckily they were easier to destroy when they weren't in the End. I hit one with a snowball and used Sean's diamond sword to strike the side of the scaly dragon. The dragon roared and then exploded.

"One down. Two to go!" Molly said as she threw a snowball at a dragon, destroying the second one.

The last dragon was strong and it was not an easy battle. We used arrows, snowballs, and diamond swords to fight the dragon, but it just didn't seem to weaken. It seemed like it had super strength. Esther used her final snowball, but the dragon didn't explode.

Molly shot arrows at the dragon, but it flew toward us and roared. I was ready to give up. I didn't have very much energy left and this was a pointless battle. We were just going to get destroyed and respawn in the prison again. This was all a part of Charles's plan.

Thao shot a final arrow at the dragon, and this time it exploded.

"Great job!" I said. "Huzzah!"

We looked over at the End portal that had spawned. Molly asked, "Should we go to the End?"

"We can't," I replied. "Our energy is so low that we would be destroyed instantly."

"We need to go to the Overworld," Esther reminded her.

"Let's build a portal," Sean said.

Luckily we had enough resources to build a portal to the Overworld, and quickly began to craft it. As we stood by the portal, ready to ignite it and finally make our way *home, Charles and his army sprinted toward us. Before we had a chance to react, they shot arrows at us, and we all respawned in our prison cells.*

When I respawned, Charles stood above me.

He laughed. "You almost made it back to the Overworld." He laughed again. "Almost."

"We are going to get out of here," I replied.

"Well, your friends aren't here anymore. I have moved them to another place. You'll never find them. So good luck trying to make it back to the Overworld on your own."

He let out another laugh and then left my cell. I was alone. It would be impossible to escape on my own. They had been so helpful. Feeling hopeless, I paced around the room and tried to come up with a plan.

A carrot came flying through the small hole in the wall. Nothing had changed.

Grabbing the carrot and chewing slowly, I began to calm down. I thought about the sword and the pickaxe I had in my inventory. I was better off than I had been before I met Sean. Maybe I could do this on my own. But I had to find my friends. Even if I didn't need them, they might need me. I stood silently and listened. I could hear muffled voices. I was sure that my friends weren't too far away, but I was shocked when they appeared in the center of my room.

"How are you here?" I asked in surprise.

"We used the potion of invisibility," explained Molly. "Remember, Thao knows the ins and outs of this place—he was able to lead us back here."

I looked over at Thao and nodded my thanks. In that moment I began to trust him. He had earned my trust.

Thao smiled. "I know another way out of here."

I was about to ask about his plan but was distracted when two blazes spawned in the center of the room. We didn't have any snowballs, and we also lacked the energy to fight them.

Thao said, "Quickly. Follow me."

We followed Thao through the hole in the wall and narrowly avoided being struck by a fireball. Thao grabbed his pickaxe and banged it against the wall. The next room contained a staircase.

"This way!" Thao said as we climbed the stairs.

There was an opening at the top of the staircase and it led to the Nether.

"We're free!" I called out.

As two ghasts flew through the sky, I held out my fist. We were together again and, together, we could do this.

13
NOBODY WINS

Good, we don't know if he returns to the stronghold. He could still be trapped in the Nether," said Harriet.

"But we still need to find him," added Jack.

"But where?" asked Ezra.

"I feel like every time we make progress, we just wind up back where we started. It's getting very tiresome." Harriet was frustrated. They had been so worried and now she just wanted to find William.

"We have to be thankful for our small victories," said Julian. "We did find Oliver."

"That's true," Harriet replied.

They were interrupted by Toby's cry. "Watch out!"

A group of ghasts and blazes flew through the sky and both of the hostile mobs shot fireballs at the group. They fought back with everything they had. They didn't want to respawn in the Overworld.

Snowballs and arrows flew through the sky. Some struck the beasts. Harriet used her fists to battle the ghasts, feeling strong when she hit a fireball and it flew back at the ghast and struck it.

Ezra and Julian threw snowballs at the blazes, destroying them. When all of the hostile mobs were destroyed, Toby said, "Wow, we are getting pretty good at this."

"Fighting is a great skill to have, but I wish we didn't have to use it," Julian remarked.

"Let's travel further into the Nether," Jack said, studying the clear sky. "It looks like we have a small break from battling hostile mobs."

As they walked past lava waterfalls and through the netherrack landscape, Harriet spotted Veronica standing alone.

"Watch out, guys. Veronica's here."

Veronica called out, "Don't worry. I'm not going to attack you. I was wondering if I could join you guys. I can't trust Valentino anymore and you guys seem a lot more trustworthy."

The gang was stunned. They didn't want to tell Veronica that they didn't trust her, that they believed this was a trap. "What happened?" asked Harriet.

"Valentino wants to destroy you guys. He wants to use command blocks to put you on Hardcore mode and destroy you. He doesn't like having you trailing us on our quest to find William," confessed Veronica.

"*Your* quest!" scoffed Harriet. "Ha!"

"And why aren't you with him?" Jack asked Veronica.

"I don't want to destroy you. I just wanted to find William first and get all the credit, but I don't want to set anyone to Hardcore mode. That would be awful."

"We aren't going to take credit for finding William. This is just about helping him return to the Overworld. Would you be okay with that?" asked Julian.

Veronica paused. "You aren't going to take credit for finding one of the most famed explorers in the Overworld? I don't understand. It doesn't make sense."

"We are only here to help free my friend. I was a prisoner for many years and it's awful. It's not about becoming famous because you found someone; it's about helping others," explained Oliver.

Veronica looked surprised. "I just thought it could be about both. You could help others and you can get credit."

The debate was cut short when a swarm of blazes flew toward them, shooting fireballs at the gang.

Veronica grabbed snowballs from her inventory and threw them at the blazes. Everybody else joined in. Harriet was about to get struck by the blaze, when Veronica pushed her out of the way.

Veronica was destroyed by the blaze, but Harriet survived.

When they had defeated all of the blazes, Harriet said, "I think Veronica has proven herself. If we see her again, we should let her join us."

The others agreed. But for now they had to move on. They had already spent a large portion of time in the Nether and right now they had no clues and were no closer to finding William.

"I see a Nether fortress," Harriet announced.

The group walked toward the Nether fortress. They were happy to see that it wasn't being guarded by blazes, and they walked right in.

They entered the temple and looked for treasure. Two magma cubes bounced toward them. Harriet took out her diamond sword and struck one of the magma cubes. The others joined in and they quickly defeated the boxy creatures.

Harriet walked toward the room where they kept the treasure and saw the two purple-helmeted treasure hunters from the Overworld.

"You are following us," one of the purple-helmeted treasure hunters called out to the group, aiming his bow and arrow.

"No. We aren't. We promise," Harriet called out.

The group didn't want to get into a fight. They just wanted to find William. Three blazes spawned in the fortress and shot fireballs at the two treasure hunters. They were destroyed instantly. The gang used their snowballs to fight the blazes. When the blazes were gone, the group walked over to the treasure chest.

Ezra opened the chest. "Look, diamonds!"

"I feel bad about taking the diamonds. The purple treasure hunters found them first," said Jack.

Veronica sprinted toward them. "I found you!"

"You just missed being attacked by two treasure hunters," Harriet told her.

"Were they wearing purple helmets?" Veronica asked.

"Yes," replied Harriet.

"They work with Valentino. They are trouble."

No longer feeling guilty, the group gathered the diamonds and placed them in their inventories. Toby spotted something on the ground next to the treasure chest. "Guys, I think I see more pages from the journal."

"I wonder if the purple-helmeted treasure hunters dropped them," said Harriet.

"Could they also be searching for William?" asked Jack.

"I'm sure they are," Veronica told them. "I told you that they work with Valentino. He has his heart set on finding William."

"We have to read the pages," said Toby.

The group gathered around and Toby read the journal aloud.

14

JOURNAL ENTRY: AN ENCOUNTER

Day 7: Encounter with Charles

We defeated the ghasts and felt confident as we traveled through the Nether.

"I think we can make it. I think we will get back to the Overworld." Molly was hopeful, and so was I.

Luckily, we had enough resources to construct a portal and we were about to craft one when a stranger approached us.

"Who are you?" I asked. I was wary of new people and just wanted us to make our way back to the Overworld without any more interruptions.

"I'm a treasure hunter. Who are you?" he asked.

"It doesn't matter," I replied. We hopped into the portal and purple mist surrounded us. Before we could stop the stranger, he had joined us. We all emerged in a grassy field in the Overworld.

"Now that you've hitched a ride with us, can you go on your way?" I asked the treasure hunter.

"Fine," he replied and darted off.

As we traveled through the grassy biome, I had a feeling we'd see him again. I wasn't going to be so friendly the next time. Spending so much time trapped in the Nether and being held prisoner had hardened me. I didn't welcome new people anymore. There was a time when I'd traveled around the Overworld and people had stopped me because I was a famous explorer and I'd spent time chatting with them. But now I had made my new friends and I just wanted to stick with them. I was so exhausted from trying to escape the Nether, that I didn't realize that we should have been celebrating. Molly reminded me.

"We're here," she said. "Finally, we're really in the Overworld. I don't believe it."

"We need to find Oliver," I told them.

"Do you have any idea where he could be?" asked Sean.

"He's in the desert. Charles accidently let that slip," I said.

"But there are many deserts in the Overworld," Esther reminded me.

"I'll search all of them if I have to. I'll search until I find him," I told the group.

"I want to go home," Molly confessed. "I don't know if I want to go on a wild goose chase for your friend. We might never find him."

"Do what you want. I'll do this alone. I can't go home until I've found my partner."

I looked out and saw cows grazing in the distance and as well as a few chickens. When I saw the chickens I realized that I was starving. It had been too long since we had eaten a proper meal.

Sean looked out and saw the chickens too. He grabbed his bow and arrow, aimed carefully, and shot a chicken on his first try. We feasted on chicken and apples that we picked from a tree. I told the others they could go their own ways—they shouldn't feel guilty. Finding Oliver was something I had to do, and I was fine doing it alone.

Esther was the first to speak. "I used to look up to you and Oliver. I would always read about your explorations. I'd be honored if you'd let me help you find your friend. I'd love to join you."

"Yes." I was thrilled. "Please join me."

Molly looked over at Esther. "I'll go too. I want to help you. I'm sorry I suggested that I wanted to abandon you."

"You don't need to apologize. You were just being honest, and you have every right to leave." I smiled.

Sean and Thao were in too. They weren't ready for the adventure to end. As my food bar replenished, I felt extremely hopeful. We would find Oliver and one day I'd be able to return to my life as an explorer.

The sun began to set and Molly suggested we build a house. We didn't have many supplies, so we built a small house rather quickly. We crawled into our beds. For the first time in a very long time, I was excited for the morning.

The morning was bright and I looked out at the sun. I had spent so long in the Nether, and the Overworld seemed even prettier than I remembered. We used some of Oliver's old maps and made our way toward the desert.

When we were in the jungle, the sky grew dark and rain started to fall on us. We tried to take shelter by a large tree, using the leaves to cover us.

"Skeletons!" Molly cried.

Skeletons were marching toward us. One of the skeletons spotted us and shot arrows.

Sean took out his bow and shot his own arrows at the skeletons, while I charged toward them with Sean's diamond sword. I was so glad to battle a mob in the Overworld. I never wanted to see another fireball. When I thought about it though, it seemed I'd grown less scared of fire, less scared of the Nether in general. I still didn't want to spend time there, but I'd gotten used to it. I'd proven I could survive there.

Our battle wasn't that hard and soon the skeletons were defeated. We picked up dropped bones and I was happy to find a dropped bow. The sun came out again and we continued our journey to the desert.

"Do you think we're going to make it?" Molly asked as we climbed up a mountain.

I stopped at the peak and pointed out the desert in the distance. "If that is the desert where Oliver is trapped, I am sure we will make it."

We climbed down the mountain and, according to Oliver's map, we were very close to the desert. We made our way through another grassy biome, and I could see the desert in the distance.

I smiled, but was surprised by a sharp pain in my arm "Ow!"

"Stop right there." The stranger who had followed us from Nether stood with his bow and arrow aimed at my chest.

"What do you want from us?" I asked him.

"I want everything in your inventory," he demanded.

"Never!" shouted Molly.

Sean took out his sword and struck the stranger. He grabbed a potion of harming and splashed it on him.

Seeing him weakened, I leapt toward the stranger and destroyed him with my diamond sword.

"How did he think he was going to win? There was only one of him and there are five of us."

Thao pointed behind us to a bunch of people dressed in black. "He wasn't alone. He's working with Charles. He probably led him to us."

I looked out at soldiers that were marching toward us. I didn't know how we'd escape. I took out my diamond sword and clutched it in my hands. I was ready for battle. This time we were out of the Nether. This time we had an advantage.

15
THE ATTACK OF THE WITHER SKELETONS

illiam isn't even in the Nether!" exclaimed Toby.

"Let's get out of here," added Jack.

Harriet surprised herself when she suggested, "Should we look for more treasure in this fortress before we go?"

"No, we have to go back to the Overworld now," Julian shouted.

Before the gang could exit the Nether fortress, a horde of wither skeletons attacked them.

Harriet struck a wither skeleton with her diamond sword, but the black skeleton of the Nether was powerful and it wasn't growing weaker.

"Help!" Harriet called out to the others, but they were all fighting their own battles. She used all of her strength to strike the wither skeleton and, just in the nick of time, she destroyed it. Harriet looked up to see another group of wither skeletons approaching them.

Jack finished battling a wither skeleton and looked up to see the new crop of skeletons. "Someone must have summoned these skeletons. We're going to have to stop this wither skeleton invasion."

"How?" Toby gasped, half out of breath, as he tried continued to battle a wither skeleton.

"I don't know, but we can't go on like this!" Julian shouted.

Harriet took some potions out of her inventory and splashed them on the skeletons. They weakened. She called to the others, "Use your potions!"

The group took out potions and threw them at the skeletons. Then they struck the weakened skeletons with their diamond swords and sprinted from the Nether fortress.

When they were out of danger, Veronica said, "We should stop here and build the portal. We have to get out of the Nether."

Quickly they crafted a portal. Purple mist rose around them as they emerged in the Overworld.

Harriet looked around the jungle where they had spawned. "Now we have to travel to the desert. I assume that's where we'll find William."

"Are you sure?" asked Jack. "Maybe he never made it to the desert."

"We need to find the next batch of missing pages from the journal," said Julian.

"You're right," said Ezra, "but I agree with Harriet— we should try to go back to search the desert. We know where they kept Oliver. Maybe William is trapped there too."

Everyone agreed and they made their way toward the desert. As they climbed up a mountain, they saw a large three-headed blue creature fly by.

"Its color is changing to black. It's the Wither boss!" cried Harriet.

The hostile mob flew by them and shot wither skulls at them. The gang dodged the skulls as they shot arrows at the three-headed beast.

"I bet Valentino summoned it!" Veronica said as she shot an arrow at the boss, striking the flying mob.

Ezra and Julian threw snowballs at the Wither. As snowballs and arrows struck it, it slowly began to lose energy.

After many hits, the Wither exploded, dropping a wither skull. Julian picked it up and placed it in his inventory. The group continued on their way down the mountain and toward the desert.

When they reached the desert, an arrow struck Julian. He looked around for the person that shot him, but he couldn't see anyone.

"Where did that arrow come from?" asked Harriet.

A voice boomed, "From me."

Valentino stood in front of them. The two purple-helmeted treasure hunters stood behind him and pointed their arrows at the gang.

"I hope you had fun fighting the Wither," one of the purple-helmeted treasure hunters said with a laugh.

"The game is over, Valentino. You need to leave us alone. You're never going to win," Julian told him.

"I see Veronica has joined you." Valentino walked over to Veronica. He put his bow and arrow back into his inventory and took out his enchanted diamond sword. He pointed it at Veronica's chest. "You're a traitor, Veronica."

"No, I'm not. I just want to do the right thing. You wanted to put these innocent people on Hardcore mode. I couldn't ever agree with that. I want to make my own choices."

"Well, you made the wrong choice." Valentino struck Veronica with his diamond sword.

Julian shot an arrow at Valentino, piercing his arm. Valentino was enraged. Together, the rest of the group attacked Valentino and the two purple-helmeted treasure hunters.

The trio was weakened. And within seconds they were destroyed. The gang sprinted toward a desert temple. As they entered the temple, they saw Valentino and the two purple-helmeted treasure hunters respawning.

"I guess this is where you are living," said Julian.

"Good guess," Valentino replied and he struck Julian with his diamond sword.

As they battled, it occurred to Julian that it was unlikely that William was still in the desert. Valentino lived here; he would have already found William if he were here. Julian realized that once this battle was over, they were going to have to start their search anew.

Outnumbered, it wasn't long before Valentino and his friends were destroyed. "Let's get out of here," shouted Julian.

He sprinted out of the desert temple and the others followed. When they were far from the desert temple and hidden by trees in the jungle, Julian told them, "I don't think William is being held prisoner in the desert."

"Why?' asked Toby.

"I think Valentino would have found him by now," he replied.

Then Ezra made an announcement, holding up some papers in his hand. "Valentino dropped these during the battle. I think they're the missing journal pages."

"That's amazing. Great job." Oliver was thrilled. "Hopefully this will bring us one step closer to finding my old friend."

The group gathered around Ezra. They wanted to know what the journal said next.

"Read it," said Veronica. "We all want to know where William is being held prisoner!"

"Do you think Valentino has read this already?" asked Jack.

"I'm not sure," Ezra replied, "but I think we still need to read it. It could help us." With that, he began to read from the journal's pages.

16
JOURNAL ENTRY: ALMOST HOME

Day 8: The Overworld

Charles called out, "It's time to give up, William."

"Never," I shouted.

"I'll give you credit, you did a good job getting out of the Nether. I didn't think you'd make it to the Overworld. But now it's over. You've lost." Charles let out another sinister laugh.

I took out my sword and leapt toward Charles. Before his army could stage an attack, Esther sprinted over to me and whispered, "Meet me in the jungle." Then she splashed a potion of invisibility on me and on the others.

We sprinted toward the jungle. When we reached the trees and began to reappear, I asked, "What should we do now? Since Charles is in the desert, I'm sure that is where Oliver is being held prisoner."

"We just need to come up with a good plan. It looks like he has a lot of soldiers in the desert." Sean paced back and forth. "How many bottles of the potion of invisibility do we have left?" he asked.

We didn't have any potion left in our inventories. We had just used the last of our stores, and we were out of spider eye. We were going to have to fight this battle without the benefit of invisibility.

"Quiet," said Esther. "I hear something."

We all stood still and listened. We could hear Charles ordering his men to find us. "Soldiers, they can't be very far from here. We have to keep looking. I won't be happy until they are destroyed. I'll put them on Hardcore mode and then we'll be rid of them all for good. Oliver, too, when we get back."

My heart beat fast. I couldn't let them destroy Oliver. I had to battle Charles. I hid behind a tree and, when Charles was in sight, I took out my diamond sword and sprinted toward him. I struck him twice and with that he was destroyed. His soldiers began to shoot arrows at me, and I sprinted as fast as I could out of the jungle.

Once I stopped sprinting, I found myself at a beach. I looked for my friends, but they weren't behind me. I had fought Charles and abandoned my friends to battle the soldiers on their own. I felt awful. I walked along the water and tried to come up with a plan. I knew I had to make my way back to the jungle and the desert. I had to find my friends.

As I walked toward the jungle, I heard a voice call out in the distance, "William."

It was Sean. I ran toward him. "I'm so happy to see you. Where are the others?"

"They're building a small house in the jungle. We defeated the soldiers and found an isolated part of the jungle where they won't find us," explained Sean.

"I feel awful for taking off after I battled Charles. I didn't mean to abandon you."

"It's okay. We all make mistakes," Sean said and he walked me toward the small jungle house.

When I entered the house, I apologized to the group. Night was setting in and everyone was crawling into bed. "It's okay," Molly said. "We just need to get some sleep. In the morning, we are going back to the desert. We will free Oliver. This battle is almost over."

I was lucky to have such great friends. I was the one who needed to find Oliver, but they were in this with me. I wouldn't abandon them again, no matter what.

I couldn't believe we were just a short distance from Oliver and that we might be able to rescue him in the morning. I could hardly sleep, I was so excited. Then I began to worry. Charles had mentioned that he was going to put Oliver on Hardcore mode. I hoped we would get there in time.

In the morning, we ate some apples and came up with a plan to defeat Charles.

I suggested summoning the Ender Dragon like Oliver and I had done in the past. Everyone agreed that was a great idea. We used command blocks and summoned several Ender Dragons to fly in the direction of the desert. This was how I defeated Charles before, and

I would do it again. We stood outside the desert and watched as the dragons flew toward them.

We could hear cries for help as the soldiers battled the Ender Dragons with arrows and snowballs. The soldiers fought very hard, but soon it went quiet. We entered the desert to survey the wreckage. Two Ender Dragons flew through the sky, and we hit them with snowballs to scare them off before moving on to explore the desert temple. We had to make sure that Charles was defeated, and we had to save Oliver.

As soon as we entered the temple, Molly asked, "Do you hear something?"

We all stopped. There was a muffled cry for help.

"I think that's Oliver!" I shouted.

We ran toward the sound of Oliver's voice, but as we turned a corner, we were ambushed by Charles, who lunged at us with his diamond sword.

"You thought you defeated me, didn't you? Well, you didn't!" Charles laughed and struck me with his sword.

My energy level was growing low. I couldn't withstand a serious battle. I didn't want to waste my energy fighting Charles—I wanted to free Oliver.

Thao struck Charles with his diamond sword.

"Hah! You think you're going to get away with this, Thao? You can never beat me." Charles let out another laugh and then called out, "Soldiers!"

A group of soldiers emerged from another room in the temple and started to attack with their diamond swords. Knowing it was a losing battle, we sprinted from the temple. This time at least we were leaving together.

"Watch out, Thao!" Molly called out.

An Ender Dragon flew down and struck Thao. He was weakened but not destroyed. I threw a snowball at the Ender Dragon and it exploded. Meanwhile a band of soldiers rushed toward us, Charles shouting, "There is no escape!"

I looked at the End portal that spawned in front of us. I called to my friends, "Hop on! We're going to the End!"

17
SLIMES AND SURPRISES

They are in the End!" Harriet called out.

"We can't be sure," said Jack. "Maybe they defeated the Ender Dragon and respawned in the Overworld."

"At least we know that William probably isn't in the desert. I don't want to go back there to fight Valentino," commented Toby.

"Did somebody say my name?" Valentino stormed over to them. He lashed out at Toby and struck him with his sword.

Ezra rushed Valentino, splashing a potion of weakness on him. Harriet hit Valentino with her diamond sword and he was destroyed.

"We have to be on the lookout for the two purple-helmeted treasure hunters." Oliver told them. "They'll be around here somewhere."

"Look!" shouted Harriet.

Everyone looked, expecting to see the two purple-helmeted treasure hunters. Instead they saw five blazes flying through the Overworld sky.

"He's summoned more Nether mobs!" cried Veronica.

"Get your snowballs out!" Julian ordered.

The group battled the yellow mobs. They threw snowballs as they dodged the fireballs that rained down on them.

Valentino must have respawned nearby. He was back, and this time he was with the two purple-helmeted treasure hunters. They attacked the group with a potion of weakness. It looked like all was lost. Weakened, they didn't have a chance against the yellow beasts from the Nether.

Harriet grabbed a potion of healing from her inventory and drank it quickly, then passed it off to her friends. With her newfound energy, she lunged toward Valentino with her diamond sword.

"You have no clue where William is," she shouted at him.

"Neither do you." He laughed. "But I know where Charles is hiding."

"What?" Harriet asked, surprised.

"Looking for me?" Charles called out.

Now they were up against Charles and Valentino together. This was their toughest challenge yet. As Harriet struck Valentino, she said, with disgust dripping from her words, "I knew you two were working together."

"Where is William?" demanded Toby, joining in the fight.

"*Stop*," roared Charles.

Surprised, everyone did as Charles had asked.

"Everyone, please put down your weapons," he continued.

Confused, it took a moment for everyone to comply. They watched each other, unsure. But Charles was the first to drop his own sword, and the others slowly followed suit.

Harriet was the last to drop her weapon. She wondered if she should strike Charles while she was at an advantage. But she didn't. That wouldn't be playing fair. Still, she was shocked that everyone had listened to him and that the fighting had stopped.

"I never saw William after he traveled to the End," Charles began. "But you have his journal. You have proof that he returned. Give us the journal."

"We did have the journal," Julian replied. "I mean, we do have the journal, but it's missing pages. We don't know where William is. We don't know if he's still in the End."

Charles looked at the group and took out his sword again. "You had better not be lying to us. If you know something and you aren't telling us or if you've hidden the missing pages, you will all suffer."

The moment of peace was broken. Harriet retrieved her own sword and struck Charles. He grabbed a potion of harming and splashed it toward her, but she jumped back. Jack gave Charles a push and Charles fell right into the potion he had intended for Harriet. He called out to his soldiers, "Help me!"

But the gang was too fast. They leapt at Charles and destroyed him. Then they battled the soldiers, Valentino, and the two purple-helmeted treasure hunters. When everyone was destroyed, Julian picked up some pages that had fluttered to the floor.

Julian said, "I think these are the final pages from the journal."

"I wonder who had them. If it was Charles or Valentino," Veronica asked.

Oliver, who was known to be extremely trusting, shocked everyone when he said, "I bet Charles and Valentino didn't even know someone had those pages. It could have been one of the treasure hunters or someone from the army. Or maybe it was one of *us*?"

They looked at one another suspiciously. Was one of them keeping secrets? Had one of them been hiding the pages?

Harriet broke the tension. "Before we start questioning everyone about the journal pages, we should read them."

And once again, Julian read out loud.

18
JOURNAL ENTRY:
IT'S THE END

Day 9: A Call for Help

If someone is reading this, I have survived the End and returned to the Overworld. Sean also respawned with me. We never saw Thao, Molly, or Esther again. We searched for them, but with Charles on the hunt for us, it became too dangerous and we went into hiding.

We felt the best way to escape was to spend time beneath the sea. We gathered potions for underwater breathing and spent a long time in an underwater temple. Sean and I changed our skins to make sure nobody would recognize us. For a while, we were safe.

But one day, a stranger appeared and in a low, familiar voice told us, "I know who you are and you can't hide any longer." He was the same man who had kept us prisoners in the Nether.

We tried to escape, but the stranger followed us wherever we went. The stranger seemed to always know our next move and found us in the jungle and the desert. As we fled, we searched for Oliver wherever we went, but we never found him.

We finally settled in a remote part of the mountains and we thought we were safe again. We lived a peaceful existence, but we missed our friends and I still hoped to find Oliver. We decided to come up with a new plan. One that would set us free from Charles and save Oliver. But that never happened. Today the stranger arrived, this time with an army wearing black robes. We fought back, but we were outnumbered. They chased us into a stronghold, one they'd kept us in before. The only way we could escape was through the portal in the End room.

I am standing in front of the portal now. My heart is beating fast and I am writing this quickly before we must return to the End and battle the Ender Dragon a second time. I hope we survive. I hope we respawn in the Overworld and that we will be placed in a location far away from the stranger and from Charles.

I will respawn. The last place I slept was the house I built in the jungle. If you find this letter, please send help!

DO YOU LIKE FICTION FOR MINECRAFTERS?

Check out other unofficial Minecrafter adventures from Sky Pony Press!

Invasion of the Overworld
MARK CHEVERTON

Battle for the Nether
MARK CHEVERTON

Confronting the Dragon
MARK CHEVERTON

Trouble in Zombie-town
MARK CHEVERTON

The Quest for the Diamond Sword
WINTER MORGAN

The Mystery of the Griefer's Mark
WINTER MORGAN

The Endermen Invasion
WINTER MORGAN

Treasure Hunters in Trouble
WINTER MORGAN

Available wherever books are sold!

LIKE OUR BOOKS FOR MINECRAFTERS?

Then check out other novels by Sky Pony Press.

Pack of Dorks
BETH VRABEL

Boys Camp: Zack's Story
CAMERON DOKEY, CRAIG ORBACK

Boys Camp: Nate's Story
KITSON JAZYNKA, CRAIG ORBACK

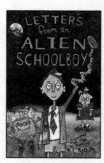

Letters from an Alien Schoolboy
R. L. ASQUITH

Just a Drop of Water
KERRY O'MALLEY CERRA

Future Flash
KITA HELMETAG MURDOCK

Sky Run
ALEX SHEARER

Mr. Big
CAROL AND MATT DEMBICKI

Available wherever books are sold!